Zac's Quicksand
published in 2014 by
Hardie Grant Egmont
Ground Floor, Building 1, 658 Church Street
Richmond, Victoria 3121, Australia
www.hardiegrantegmont.com.au

A CiP record for this title is available from the National Library of Australia.

Illustrations by Tomomi Sarafov
Design by Stephanie Spartels

1 3 5 7 9 10 8 6 4 2

Printed in China by WKT Company Ltd.

ZAC'S QUICKSAND

BY H.I. LARRY

ILLUSTRATIONS BY TOMOMI SARAFOV

hardie grant EGMONT

CHAPTER

Zac Power was at the beach for the weekend. It was one of Zac's favourite spots.

The beach had big sand dunes. The surf was always good.

And there was a shop that sold the best burgers.

Zac was 12 years old. He was a spy. All of his family were spies too. They did top-secret work for the good spy group GIB.

Zac went on cool missions for GIB. He worked hard to stop the evil spy group BIG.

GIB spies had code names.

Zac's code name was Agent Rock Star.

Zac's brother Leon was in charge of the GIB Test Labs. He made loads of spy gadgets and vehicles. It was Zac's job to test them.

Zac was getting hot at the beach. He went inside to play a computer game.

The computer game was called Mega Maze. Zac was at the top level. On the screen, Zac was racing at high speed.

I'm winning, thought Zac.

I'm going to be the best maze racer of all time!

Zac was close to the maze exit. He turned right down the last tunnel. He raced towards the end of the maze. Suddenly the screen went black.

Oh no, thought Zac. *I didn't get to save my game!*

He picked up the TV remote.

Before he could push anything

the TV screen flashed.

Zac took his GIB SpyPad

from his pocket. The SpyPad

was a phone and a computer.

Zac could record music on it.

And it had all the latest games.

There were three missed calls

on Zac's SpyPad.

There was also a message

from Leon.

Urgent test driving needed.

Come to the Sand Crawler

Centre.

Awesome! thought Zac.

CHAPTER

Zac headed out the door.

The Sand Crawler Centre

was over some sand dunes.

He knew exactly where to go.

Zac LOVED sand crawling.

He ran all the way there.

Zac was puffed when he reached the centre. It was super-busy.

I hope Leon wants me to do some sand crawling, thought Zac.

Zac went over to the sand crawlers. They had skis on the front. There were tracks at the back. The tracks spun around to move the crawler along.

Crawlers were perfect for racing over sand dunes. Zac had ridden them loads of times.

People hired sand crawlers from the centre.

There are only two left, thought

Zac. *But the sand dunes are empty.*

Where is everyone?

Zac felt someone grab his

arm. It was Leon. He looked

grumpy. 'Why didn't you

answer your SpyPad, Zac?'

asked Leon.

'I was playing Mega Maze,' said

Zac. 'I didn't hear my SpyPad.'

'I'd be the best maze driver ever if you hadn't sent that message,' Zac said grumpily.

'Well, I had to get hold of you somehow,' said Leon.

'Do I get to ride a sand crawler?' asked Zac.

Just then Zac's SpyPad beeped. It was a message from GIB.

Sand crawler riders are going missing.

You need to find out what's happening to them.

'I need you to test drive two

gadgets on your mission,'

said Leon.

Leon and Zac walked outside.
They went over to a wall of
thick bush and palm trees.

Leon took out his SpyPad and
pushed some buttons.

The wall of trees began to
move apart. They slid open to
make a doorway. There was a
secret room behind them!

'Awesome hiding place,' said Zac.

'You'd never know this room was here.'

Zac and Leon walked through the door. The trees closed quickly behind them.

CHAPTER 3

'This is the latest GIB Test

Lab,' said Leon.

Zac looked around. There

were computers and gadgets

everywhere.

In the corner was a glass case with some very cool-looking watches.

Leon opened the case.
He took out an orange watch with a silver band. He handed it to Zac. 'This is the E-10 GPS Watch,' said Leon.

'Cool,' said Zac. Zac put the watch on his wrist. 'What does it do?' he asked Leon.

'It will tell you where to go if you get lost,' said Leon. 'It's also a phone.'

'Awesome,' said Zac.

'I need you to test the phone,' said Leon. 'Use the watch to call me instead of your SpyPad.'

'OK,' said Zac.

'The face of the watch opens too,' said Leon.

Zac popped open the face of the watch. There was a packet of gum inside.

'It's De-Fog Gum, Zac,' said Leon. 'It clears your head and wakes you up when your brain feels foggy.'

'Cool,' said Zac.

'One piece will wake you up for three minutes. Then it stops working.' Leon opened a door at the back of the lab.

Behind the door stood a sand crawler. It was blue and gold with red flames.

Zac had never seen a cooler sand crawler.

'This is the Speed–Ski Super Crawler,' said Leon. 'It's the fastest sand crawler ever.'

Leon pushed more buttons on his SpyPad. The door to the Test Lab opened up.

'You'd better get going, Zac,' said Leon. 'And make sure you do your test drive report.'

Zac groaned.

He loved test driving but he
hated doing reports.

'I know, I know,' said Zac.

Zac jumped on the Super
Crawler.

He turned the grips on the
Super Crawler's handle-bars.
The engine roared to life.
The Super Crawler shot
out the door and up the
sand dunes.

CHAPTER

The Super Crawler flew over the first dune. *This is SO cool,* thought Zac. Then he heard a beeping noise.

It was coming from his watch.

Leon's face popped up on the watch.

'Just testing out the watch, Zac. Have you seen anything yet?' asked Leon.

'No,' said Zac. 'There's no-one out here.'

'GIB think BIG know about the Super Crawler,' said Leon. 'They want to steal it and copy it.'

'Do they know I'm riding it?' asked Zac.

'No, Zac,' said Leon. 'But they are taking every crawler they find until they get the one they want.'

'But what have they done with the riders on the other crawlers?' said Zac.

'We don't know,' said Leon.

'I'm going up to the top of the biggest sand dune,' said Zac. 'I'll be able to see better from there.'

Zac reached the top of the dune and looked around.

'There's nothing to see, Leon,' said Zac.

Suddenly, Zac was falling. The Super Crawler was sinking through the sand. It was quicksand!

'Leon, I'm –'

But Zac was already up to his neck in the sand. His watch went dead. Leon was gone.

Zac tried to climb out of the sand. But that just made him sink even deeper.

He could hear the crawler's tracks whirring. Quicksand was flying everywhere. But Zac kept sinking.

He took a big breath as the crawler sank down into the quicksand.

Suddenly, Zac was falling
through the air. He landed
with a THUMP!

He had gone through the
quicksand and now he was
in a dark space.

Zac turned on the Super Crawler's lights.

Zac was in a tunnel. He drove along it. Up ahead, there were lots more tunnels. They all went in different directions.

Zac had to choose which way to go. *It's an underground maze,* he thought. *Maybe my GPS watch can help me get out.*

Zac checked his watch.

The screen was black. *Oh no!* thought Zac. *It doesn't work underground. I'll have to work out the maze myself.*

Zac drove down some tunnels but everything looked the same.

Zac noticed a strange smell in the air. It was getting stronger.

CHAPTER 5

Zac turned right. He was in a big room. It was full of people on crawlers.

The drivers were driving very slowly.

Zac's brain started to feel foggy. *The air in here is terrible,* he thought. He sniffed the air. *I know this smell! It's BIG gas!! It makes people sleepy.*

Zac needed to do something fast. Suddenly he thought of the De-Fog Gum.

He popped open the face of his watch. Zac took out the De-Fog Gum and chewed.

It tastes just like strawberries!

thought Zac. *Yum!*

Zac stopped feeling sleepy.

The gum was working.

Zac had 11 pieces of gum left.
He counted the riders.

Phew! he thought. *Just enough for each rider to have a piece.*

Zac rode up to each rider.
He gave them a piece of
De-Fog Gum. All the riders
began waking up.

'The De-Fog Gum only lasts
for three minutes,' said Zac.

'Then we'll all start falling asleep again. Follow me. Hurry!'

CHAPTER

Zac led the riders down some
more tunnels. He looked
around. *This is just like my
Mega Maze game*, he thought.
I know exactly where to go now!

Zac sped up another tunnel.
He checked to see that
everyone was following him.

He turned right, then left, then
left again.

I'm sure this is the way out,
thought Zac.

He turned left again. *The exit is
at the end of the tunnel to the right,*
he thought.

Zac took the next turn to the right. At the end of the tunnel was a rock wall.

Everyone behind Zac stopped. Zac kept riding. He was headed straight for the rock wall.

'Come on,' yelled Zac. 'There's a secret tunnel up here!'

At least, I hope there is! he thought.

The riders started following him again.

Zac was just about to hit the wall when he turned right. He drove up a ramp and on to the beach.

Lucky I played Mega Maze! Zac thought. *I knew there was a hidden tunnel right at the very end.*

Everyone had followed him. Zac looked around for BIG agents. But there was no-one around.

Suddenly Zac's watch beeped. It was Leon calling.

'Well done, Zac,' said Leon.

'Come back to the Sand Crawler Centre.'

'OK,' said Zac. *But not before I take this Speed-Ski Super Crawler for a real spin on the dunes,* Zac thought.

'And Zac,' said Leon, 'Where is my test drive report?'

Zac turned the watch off and groaned.

THE END

TEST DRIVE
REPORT

E-10 GPS Watch

The De-Fog gum was brilliant.
The watch didn't work underground, though.

Speed-Ski Super Crawler

This crawler looks great but it's useless
in quicksand. The tracks did nothing.
But the lights were very handy.